Retaliation

II

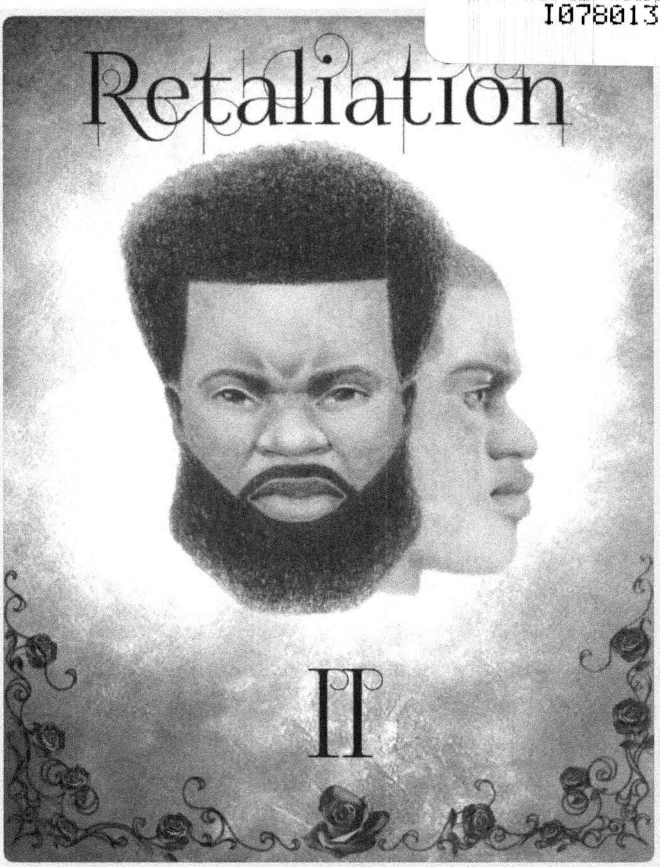

A few years later, Richard and the twins were still anguished about Teresa's death. Richard couldn't comprehend why someone would want to kill his wife. The twins still didn't understand why mommy wasn't coming home anymore. Everyone in town was still grieving, including family and friends. No one understood why something like this would happen to one of the most thoughtful, caring, compassionate people you could ever meet. Everyone still came together for Richard and the twins. They took turns cooking and cleaning, but after everything settled down, the pain continued to kick in.

The twins stayed in their room a lot and cried. Richard remained perched on the couch downstairs watching old wedding videos of him and Teresa with a pint of tequila. Richard became an alcoholic and drank from morning to night. He was even incapable of running his own company.

The family tried to talk to him about his drinking and he promised them that he would stop. Instead of listening to their suggestions, he decided to just hire a housemaid so they wouldn't have to come over as much. He told his family that he hired someone to look after him and the twins, so he didn't need them to come over anymore.

One morning, Richard's secretary Tammy became so worried about him because he hadn't answered his phone for days. She decided to call his bishop to tell him about her concern. Bishop Mike II decided to go over to Richard's house to check on him and the twins.

As he drove down their street, he noticed the twins walking towards him and he stopped. He told them to get in the car. They were crying so hard that it made the bishop start crying. He asked them, "where are they going?" They told him they were going to heaven to find their mom.

When they got out of the car, Bishop just looked at them and gave them a hug and said, "You will see your mom again, but not right now. God needed her in heaven."

The twins said together, "We needed her down here too," and ran into the house. As the Bishop walked behind the twins, he saw Richard laying on the couch drunk. Bishop told the twins to go upstairs to unpack their stuff while he got Richard up. The housemaid had no idea the twins were gone. She was downstairs in the basement washing clothes.

When the Bishop finally woke Richard up, he said, "Get it together, Richard! The twins need you."

Richard started crying uncontrollably, until the Bishop started to pray for him. Shortly after he prayed for him, Richard started muttering about how he didn't treat his wife the way God wanted him to. He told the bishop, "I thought as long as I was paying the bills and giving her and the twins what they wanted, I was doing my job as a husband."

Bishop said, "I understand. Sometimes we don't know if we weren't taught it or see our fathers do it. That's why a lot of men don't know." He continued, "I wasn't the perfect husband either until. I started going to church and getting closer to God, learning more about the bible, finding out what God wanted instead of what I desired. You can't go back and change what you didn't do in the past. But right now brother, you have to be there more than anything for the twins."

Richard hugged the Bishop. The Bishop said, "We will be there for you and the blessings that God has given you and Teresa." As the Bishop left, Richard went upstairs to take a shower. After his shower, he went to the twin's room to tell them how sorry he was and gave them a tight hug, as though he was holding them for dear life. They all started crying to the point where the twins became sick. Richard lay down with them until they fell asleep.

After they fell asleep, Richard went downstairs and threw away all of the alcohol that was in the house. He then called his secretary and said, "Thank you for always being there for me. I'm sorry for not answering your phone calls." "It's okay. I understand because you and the twins have been through a lot. That's what families do. "I'll be coming back into work Monday morning." After they hung up, Richard began to pray and repent for everything he did.

Richard and the twins began to go to counseling at the church with Bishop Mike II. They still wake up calling for their mom, but no one answers. Tonight, Richard hears them screaming that the person that killed their mother is in the house. Richard runs into their room and tells them it's going to be okay, "Mom is in heaven watching over us."

They said, "We know Dad, but he is in both of our dreams. He is in the house." Richard said, "No, he isn't babies. He just hugged both of them and told them it was going to be okay. "Come on, let's go to my room. You can sleep with dad." They looked at him and said, "Ok, dad. We love you." He told them "I love you too." "Your mom didn't get killed babies, she died from pneumonia." We know Dad, but in our dreams, that's what happened."

The next morning, Richard was up fixing breakfast and getting ready for work when he asked the twins, "What do you want for breakfast?" They both said at the same time, "waffles, eggs, strawberries, and whipped cream." This is what their mom used to make for them. They have been eating the same thing since their mom was killed. As Richard put the finishing touches on breakfast, he told the twins to eat before the school bus came. While Richard went upstairs to finish getting ready for work, he looked in the mirror where there was a picture he kept of Teresa. He said to himself, "Honey, I wish I knew then what I know now. I would have never done you and the kids like this. I truly messed up our lives. I wish it was me instead of you, baby." He began crying and said, "God,

I am so sorry for not appreciating the angel you put into my life." The twins came running up the stairs saying, "Let's finish getting ready for school," when they saw their daddy crying. "What's wrong dad?" He replies, "There is something in my eye." He did not want them to see him crying. Justin said, "Dad, I can blow in your eye like mom used to do when we had something in our eye."

Richard started laughing, "It is okay now baby. Go get on the bus before you miss it." "Okay, daddy," and they gave Richard a hug and told him they loved him. "I love you more. See you when you get out of school." Richard continued to get ready for work. When he finally made it there, he opened the door to his office and was greeted by his secretary Tammy.

"How are you doing today Mr. Williams?"

"I'm blessed."

"Me too, Mr. Williams. Your coffee is on your desk with the new contract." Richard heads over to his desk to review the contract for remodeling the church basement that he attends. While he is going over the contract, his secretary tells him someone is waiting for him for an interview. It was a young man, Tom, from the church that he's been trying to help. The young man had a rough childhood growing up. His dad was not in his life and his mom was on drugs. Richard is like a big brother to him. He made sure the young man had food, clothes, and somewhere to live. He told Richard in the interview that he just wanted to take care of his child. His mother and father were not there for him. Richard told Tom that he understood. After the interview, they both smiled. Richard gave him a hug and Tom left.

After a long day at work, Richard made it home just in time before the kids made it there. Richard said to himself, "I underestimated Teresa. She was truly a blessing from God. I didn't know half of what I had. She did so much, God. I wish I could go back and change what I did." Crying, he said, "Help me, God. Please, this is truly hard. I thought it would get easier." He heard a voice, "What does it profit a man to gain the whole word but lose his own soul? Richard said, "I know, God. All those women weren't worth the one woman that you blessed me with. I am sorry, Father. I thought that it would be easy by now, but it's not. Please help me, God."

The twins walked through the door. Justice said, "Mom, Mom, we're here. Oh, Mom's not here." Justin said, "She's in heaven watching over us." With that, they both hugged each other and started crying. Richard walked into the room and hugged them. He said, "I know it's hard, but we will be okay. God has us." The twins went upstairs and put their books away and freshened up for the dinner that Richard made. When they came downstairs, Justice said, "Some kids were talking about you and mom." Richard asked, "What did they say?" "They said mom died from AIDS." "Don't believe what you hear. I told you all what happened to your mom when you were younger." Justice said, "What did you say dad? We don't remember." "She died from pneumonia."

They said, "That's not what we heard. Dad, what really happened to mom?" Crying, Richard said, "What happened to her?" I told you what happened to her. Now go upstairs until I fix your plates." The twins went upstairs to their room. They began searching the internet to find out what really happened to their mother. They searched for their mother's name and her face popped up. They came across the newspaper article with the story that they found her shot to death at a hotel by someone and they are still looking for her killer.

They were so shocked as they continued to read the horrifying things that were said. The twins couldn't stop crying and trembling. They couldn't catch their breath. They didn't understand as they both looked at each other with their mouths open trying to grasp what they had just read. Justice threw their laptop to the floor and started tearing up their room.

Richard was already going up the stairs to talk to them about what was going on at school, when he heard the commotion and glass breaking. Justin was so angry; he threw the laptop at the window and broke it. As Richard burst through the door, he saw their room was torn up. He didn't understand why they would do this. He yelled, "What is wrong with y'all? I told you don't believe what you hear at your school. There have been so many lies going on that I just want us to just heal from all of this." Justin said, "They are not the only ones lying." "What did you say?"

Justin said, "Nothing." The twins looked at Richard frowning and said, "Whatever." He told them, "I am your dad, and you all are going to watch what you say to me in my house." Richard then told them it was time for dinner.

Richard closed their door and said to himself, "I am going to have to tell them the truth God, one day, but I don't know where to start, knowing it was because of me. She would still be here." The twins came downstairs to eat dinner. It was quiet at the table. Richard was the only one talking. After they ate, they went upstairs to get ready for bed. Richard stayed downstairs to clean up. When he went upstairs to get ready for bed, he said his prayers first and then went to sleep.

2

Richard began to make breakfast for the twins, but they said they didn't want anything to eat. He said, "What is wrong?" They told him, "Nothing."

"You have to eat something." They both grabbed an apple and left without giving their dad a hug. Richard asked, "No hug, babies?" The twins said, "Don't want to miss the bus, Richard."

"My name is dad." They just continued to walk out the door. Richard said to himself, What is going on with the twins? They have never called me by my first name before.

When Richard got to work, George was waiting for him. He hadn't seen him in years and was surprised to see him. Richard hugged George and said, "Where have you been? I haven't seen you since Teresa's funeral."

"I had to go out of town for personal reasons."

"Okay, are you working?" George said, "I have a part time job."

"Do you like it?"

"It is okay for what I need to do."

"What shift do you work?"

"Nights."

"Oh, okay. I would really like to hire you for the new job I have coming up, George. Would you like to work for me again?" "Yes, that would help even more, but I still want to do my other job." Richard said, "that's okay, I just know you are a good worker."

"Thanks man I needed that." They hugged and Richard told George, "I will give you a call Monday morning with all the information about the new job." George said thanks again man. I am really sorry about your wife Teresa. She seemed like she was the glue that was holding your family together.

"She was." George started to hug him again and said "if you need me brother for anything I'm here."

"Thanks again, it's been truly hard."

"I just can't imagine what you've been going through brother." I couldn't have gone through this if it wasn't for God. George said Amen to that brother. Well, I have to go get ready for work." Okay man love you brother." Love you too.

Richard didn't feel like cooking and brought a pizza home for dinner. The twins walked through the front door while Richard was upstairs taking a shower. Justice said "oh I see he bought pizza again. I'm so tired of pizza." Laughing out loud Justin said "We are going to turn into a pizza." Richard came down the stairs and said, "Hey what's so funny?" Justin said "Nothing," and they walked past their dad and went upstairs. Richard told them, "Make sure you all find something to wear to church for Sunday."

"Okay, Richard," Justice said.

"Didn't I tell you not to call me that!"

"Yes sir, okay," said the twins at the same time and smiled at one another, as they looked for something to wear.

Richard's phone went off. It was George. He said, "What are you doing, brother?" Richard said, "Nothing right now, just relaxing."

"Do you want to go out for a drink?"

"Brother, those days are over."

"Why don't you go out anymore, man?"

"I have not since Teresa passed. I stopped all that. I just started going to church more, with my twins. You know that was the best thing that ever happened to me. It really helped me and the twins to attend church. We also have been getting counseling from my Bishop Mike II."

"What is the name of the church?" Deliverance and Healing Home of God."

"Oh, okay. I have never been to church in my life."

"Well, I would like to invite you to stop by and check it out."

"Okay, text me the address and the time service starts. I just might come. After George hung up the phone and started laughing out loud, he said to himself why not go to church? Who knows brother might get healed, deliver and also find wife number two, smiling then said. I am really enjoying this brotherly love relationship. As he began to watch television with a "Devious" look on his face. George looked at his watch and decided that he was going out to this club about an hour away from where he lives to go have a few drinks. George put on a white suit, black button down shirt with some black snakeskin shoes, his expensive watch and his jewelry. When he finally makes it to the club, he pulls up in a black Bentley with white interior, and gives his keys to the valet. He walks up to the front of the club where the bouncer lets him in. "Why everyone else still have to wait in line?" One of the young ladies that were standing in line said to George. "Oh you got it like that?" He smiled and continued to walk in, going straight to the bar to sit down. George ordered himself a drink. The young ladies finally made it in the club. They walked over to where George was and started to order their drinks. He told the bartender that he was paying for their drinks. One of the young ladies said, "Are you paying for all our drinks?" "Yes," he responded. She then said "thank you." George told her "no problem, anytime." He turned back around, and finished enjoying his beverage, while listening to the music. Hours later….the ladies were drunk. One of the women came back to the bar and sat next to Geoge. "He asked her if he could buy her another drink." "She shook her head then said, "Of course thank you." Then she asked George, "What's your name?" He said, Sam. "She said, " You don't look like a Sam." "George said, "What do I look like?" She told him, you look more like a Rayhem. He started laughing. The young woman said her name was Neisha. That's a pretty name for a beautiful Queen. She said thank you, then smiled. "Let's get out of here." "George asked, where do you want to go? And she responds, anywhere you are going. "He said baby girl you don't even know me, and what about your friends? They will be fine. "He told her," Trust me, you don't want to open up this Pandora box, "she smiled and said yes. "I like opening up boxes, especially when they are wrapped up like you." He laughed, and told her not this box baby.

  Then Neisha went over to tell her friends and sister that she was leaving with Sam. Neisha's sister told her we came together and we are going to leave together! She told them "Not tonight, with a smirk on her face." Her sister said, "What is wrong with you, Neisha, you do this every time we go out. Plus, you are getting married next month. That's why, I need to test the water one more time, before being trapped with one man for the rest of my life, "Sister." Sam is probably not his real name anyway and Neisha might not be my real name either. She started laughing and just walked toward George. "Let's go." He asked "Are you sure you want to leave with a stranger?" "Neisha said, of course." He told her to lead the way. The valet gets George's car and they leave. Her sister finally comes outside trying to stop her. Unfortunately, they are already gone.

 "He asked her," What do you want to do? "She said "You." George laughed, and told her again "Are you sure you want to open this box up?" The young lady said, "Yes I do, but I'm not the only one opening up a box. Smiling....she said, " you are too." They started laughing. "He told her everything that looks good to you baby isn't always good for you. George is still smiling at her. "He then asked her, "where do you want to go, because I'm not from here?" She told him about a hotel around the corner from the club. After they got in the room, George put on some protection, but the condom broke. He tried to get up. It was too late. She said "It's cool, "I'm on the pill anyway. " He just looked at her and shook his head.

They went to take a shower before leaving the room. He opened the car door for her, then George got in the car. Neisha asked George for his number, and he gave it to her. He then takes her back to the club, where the ladies were still waiting. George said to himself "I warned her over and over again, but she just didn't listen to brother....just like a woman. "Laughing, " He said, "You live by the sword, you die by the sword." Three weeks later, Neisha woke up throwing up. She called Dr. Shayeen Edwards to see if it was okay for her to come in. The doctor said, yes because there was a cancellation, but Neisha needed to come in now. When she finally made it, they asked her to take a pregnancy test? "I know I'm not pregnant", she said with an attitude. I'm on the pill. Let's make sure since you've been throwing up, also let's do blood work. The results came 24 hours later. Dr. Shayeen Edwards called Neisha and told her to come back into the office "Why do I have to come in? " I have to give you your results in person." "What is the problem? I'm Pregnant? Neisha started crying on the phone. She said, "okay on my way." When she made it there, the doctor told her she was pregnant and she had HIV. Neisha fell to the floor shaking and crying uncontrollably, but how did I catch HIV? Maybe you need to discuss that with your sex partner.

He also needs to come in for blood work as well. She knew that her fiance was still a virgin; he was just waiting until they got married. That is when she thought to herself Sam, he warned me not to do it, but I was so stupid, ignorant and drunk I didn't listen to him. She decided to call the number that George gave her, but it was disconnected. She kept calling over and over again, but still the same message. The number was no longer in service. Neisha decided to go back to the club where she met George and asked the bartender that worked that night if he had seen him. The bartender told her "no, he hadn't seen him since that night." "Smiling, he said, you were all over him like you were the paparazzi. Neisha didn't know what she was going to tell her fiance, so she went back home to pack up all her clothes before he got off work. Neisha decided to leave a letter explaining what happened with Sam that night; also telling him about her test result, saying how sorry she was for not being the woman that he deserves.

When he made it home and read the letter, he tried to call her, but there was no answer. He called again and again. Finally, it went straight to voicemail. He decided to call her family to tell them about the letter. They called the police station, but there was nothing that could be done because Neisha is an adult and she left a letter saying she was not coming back. Nevertheless, the family still had her picture posted on social media and put up posters all over the city. They still couldn't find her. They looked for years, but never found Neisha. Her sister and friends continued to go to the same club every weekend, thinking that Sam was going to be there.

Five years later, Her sister got a call from a private number. She looked at the phone, and laughingly said, "This must be a bill collector because I haven't paid my student loan back. "The phone rings again. She decided to answer it, she said hello. There was no response. Hello….still there was no response. Then she said I know this isn't my baby dad's girlfriend playing on my phone again. Just when she was about to hang up. Neisha told her, it's me, your sister. Me and the baby are okay. I had a girl named Miracle. She wasn't born with HIV. Her sister started crying, saying thank you God, telling Neisha how much they love her and miss her. Then she asked where they lived. Neisha told her don't worry about us, we are okay, love you sister and hung up the phone immediately. Her sister just sat there and started trembling, crying uncontrollably.

3

Richard and the twins were getting ready for church, but they were taking longer than usual. Richard went into their room to see if he could get them to move faster. Richard said,

"What is going on with you all today?"

"Nothing, dad."

"Well, get ready before we are late for the bishop's sermon." When they finally made it to church, the bishop just walked up to the pulpit. The Bishop said, "Amen, church." The members said, "Amen, Bishop."

"I can't hear your amen, church."

"Amen!"

"That's what I'm talking about!"

As the Bishop started talking about forgiveness, George walked through the church doors. "There is nothing like forgiveness. Can I get an amen, church? Colossians 3:13 Bear with each other and forgive one another if any of you has a grievance against someone. Forgive as the Lord forgave you." How do we expect God to forgive us, when we can't forgive our brother or sister?" Richard looked around as the bishop was preaching and saw George looking around for him. They finally saw each other. Bishop Mike II continued, "Yes, we must forgive to heal our mind, body and soul. Without forgiveness, how are we going to make it through those pearly gates? Amen. Even when Jesus was nailed to the cross, Luke 23:34 He still said Father, forgive them, for they don't know what they are doing." He still was willing to forgive us. Jesus has been through it. This is why God sent His only begotten son. I mean ONLY son to die for our sins. We didn't even deserve it, but he loved us that much. God has us through the good, bad, and the ugly. Can I get an Amen? Well, I can't end this service without asking. Does anyone want to give their life to God? We don't know the time nor the hour when Jesus will come back to get His bride of the Church without spots or wrinkles."

The Bishop said to the church, "I have been where you are. I haven't always been the person I am now. I had to wake up and smell the coffee. I had to stop straddling the fence. I had a rash so bad from straddling. The fence cream couldn't even heal it, only God could. I smoked so much marijuana I should have looked like a marijuana plant. I drank so much I should have been peeing gin. God did not give up on me. He was still there for me. When everyone else forgot about me, God didn't! Hallelujah! God said it is time. Amen." Twenty people were saved that day. After the church service, members gathered outside. Bishop Mike II saw Richard and the twins. He walked over to Richard and asked him, "How are you and the twins doing?"

Richard responded, "Blessed thanks to God and the members of the church." Then George walked up, and Richard introduced him to the bishop. Richard said, "Bishop, this is George, a very good friend of mine. He just came back to town. I also hired him for the church project."

"Amen, brother," the bishop said. "I hope to see you again, brother. I feel like you have a lot on your mind. You can always come and talk to me if you need to. I want to welcome you back, brother George."

"Well thanks Bishop, but I am good."

"Just know God knows your heart. You all have a blessed day. They were walking to their cars when Richard asked George, "Are you okay?"

"Yes, brother, I'm good. I just have never been to church." Richard asked, "Why not?"

"I have my reasons."

"God showed me how much He loves me." George said, "Even after Teresa got killed? You still believe in God?" "Yes, evil still exists, as well as good. I just wish I believed sooner. She would still be here."

"It is not your fault she got killed."

"Yes, it is, George."

"What do you mean Richard?"

"I do not want to talk about it, okay?" As Richard walked away, he told George he would see him at work Monday morning.

Monday Morning….

At work, Richard told George what he needed him to do on the job. George said, "Ok. What did you mean it was your fault? What happened to your wife?" Richard said, "Didn't I tell you that I don't want to talk about it. George, if I got to hear this when I am around you, this isn't going to work." Richard walked away mad. George laughed to himself, "Maybe if she kept her legs closed, she would have been here." Later in the day, George got ready for his second job.

On death row, Lisa became a big influence on the other inmates. She became a woman of God again. She held Bible studies and talked to them about how God has been such a blessing in her life, how. He healed her from an incurable disease, and how God has forgiven her for her past life. As the women were listening to the sister of God talk about the goodness of God, the top corrections officer sat in the corner, smiling as he watched her. The inmates gave her the name Sister because she had been teaching them about the word of God. When she was through teaching the inmates, C.O. Big Lee walked over to her and said, "Amen, sister," as he clapped his hands and smiled. He does this every time without fail. She said, "Hey, Officer Big Lee."

"Hey, Sister. How are you doing?"

"Blessed."

"You are really teaching these inmates about God. That is so good. Maybe when they get out of prison, they will not make the same mistake that got them in here." Sister asked, "How did you get the name Big Lee?" He laughed, "Do you need to ask that? Look at me."

"Well, you are right about that. You are a big man."Big Lee said, "I got that name when I started working here. They said it is because of my size" Oh."Then he asked her, "How did you get your name?"

"It is a long story."

Big Lee said, "Well, it's not like you don't have the time to tell me." They both started laughing. She said, "Because I started teaching the inmates about God's word. How he is a healer and a forgiving God. They said I act like a big sister to them." She laughed.

 "Oh," he said, "Well, if you need anything, I do mean anything sister. I got you." He smiled.

"Thanks Officer Big Lee." Big Lee walked away so that he could clock out and go home.

Next Day....

George showed up at his job at the church. The Bishop saw him working. He said, "Hello, George. It's good to see you again."

"It's good to see you too, Bishop Mike II."

"Did you like the service Sunday?"

"Yes, it was nice."

"You are welcome to come again if you like." George replied, "No thanks."

"Okay, just letting you know. Whenever you are ready because God will never leave you nor forsake you, brother."

"Thanks Bishop, but I need to finish up before my boss gets here."

"Okay, you have a blessed day."

"You too."

Laughing, George said to himself, "Why does he keep trying to get me to come back to church. Does he understand English are Ebonics? I don't go to church." Richard showed up at the job to tell George he could go for the day and that he did a great job. "Please come back tomorrow." George said, "Okay," as he started to walk away. He then said, "Hey, let's do lunch one day." "Okay, George, but I'm in a hurry right now. I gotta get home before the twins get out of school."

"I understand brother, maybe tomorrow, okay?" Richard made it home to get dinner ready for the twins. They walked through the door and went upstairs to put their books away. Richard said, "Hello," and they kept walking. Richard said, "Did you hear me?" They said, "Hello, dad," with an attitude.

"What is wrong with you all?" The twins responded, "Nothing, dad."

"Well, something is wrong. You guys have been coming home with an attitude."

"We miss our mom."

Richard started crying and said, "I know. I miss her too."

"The kids kept telling us about our mom today, Dad." Richard just held his head down and said, "I will be coming up to your school tomorrow." The twins said, "No, dad. You will make it worse. We will be okay." Richard said to himself, "I am going to have to tell them everything that happened." The twins sat at the table as they finished eating dinner. They went upstairs to their room and Justice said, "Why won't dad just tell us the truth about mom?" Justin said, "Maybe he doesn't want us to be ashamed of her." They cried as they hugged each other until they fell asleep.

At the prison, Sister and the other inmates were eating dinner when Officer Big Lee walked into the cafeteria. He sat back and waited until they got through. The first thing he did was give Sister some magazines. She said, "Thanks, but you didn't have to do this, Officer Big Lee." He told her, "I wanted to. You do so much for everybody else. I just wanted to do something for you, Sister."

"Thanks." She started to walk away when she stopped and turned around to ask him, "What is your full name?" He told her he didn't like it and that is why he just used part of it. "Oh," and she walked away. He then started to finish up his rounds before his shift ended.

George and Richard were at work trying to finish up the church project. George said, "Hey, do you think we can go out to lunch?" Richard responded, "Yes, we can. "They went out to lunch at a restaurant around the corner from the job. A young waitress came over to take their order. They told her what they wanted. When the waitress left, George said to Richard, "I wish she was on the menu," laughing. "I would love to take her home." Richard said, "Aren't you married, right?"

"When I am with her, I'm married, but by myself, I'm not," George said laughing. Richard said, "That is exactly why my marriage was messed up."

"What are you talking about, Richard?"

"I'd rather not talk about it." George asked, "Why not? If it was on you, man, maybe you can help me from being a part-time husband," he said laughing.

"I don't want to talk about it." George continued, "Well, I was at my other job on lunch break and the word on the street is that your wife and another woman were having sex with different men and gave them AIDS. They found her in a hotel, shot in the head, lying on the bed with a black rose on the side of her. On the other side, there was a tombstone saying

"Revenge. "Richard told him, "Don't believe everything you hear." Angry, Richard hopped up and left his money on the table while George sat there laughing.

They both returned to the job site. It was so quiet for the rest of the day you could cut the tension with a knife. When the day was over, Richard got in his car and said to himself, "Now, how did he know all that? It wasn't in the newspaper. They just said she was killed. They did not give details about her murder. I don't trust him. I am going to speed up the progress and complete this job sooner. Richard called more workers to help him finish up."

The Next Day....

George and Richard were already at work when more workers walked in. George seemed confused and said, "Oh, we have more workers?" Richard responded, "Yep, the bishop wants to get done sooner than he contracted it for."
"Okay, you are the boss."

Three weeks later, they were done with the job. George said to Richard, "What is the next project?" He told him, "I will give you a call when I need you."

"Thanks." Richard made it home before the twins. When they came in, he told them, "We need to talk." They said, "Okay, dad." Richard sat the twins down to tell them everything. He said, "You are older now and you all need to know the truth of what happened." As Richard started to tell them about what happened to their mom, the twins started to cry uncontrollably. "It's all my fault what happened to your mom."

He continued to tell them how he cheated on Teresa with all types of women without being safe. I thought as long as I was providing for you that was all I had to do. Your mom was a good mother and a good wife." The twins were so mad at him that they both started to attack him. He couldn't control them. Justin hit Richard in the eye so hard and that's when Richard finally stood up. He grabbed both of them and held them down until they stopped fighting him.

"I'm so sorry," Richard repeated over and over again. They started running up the stairs and told Richard they hated him. He ran after them, but they locked the door to their room. He told them, "When you want to talk some more, we can."The twins did not come out of their room the entire weekend, not even to eat. Richard put the food outside of the door, he knocked on their bedroom door to tell them he was not going to work, and they did not have to go to school. He wanted to give them more time so they could talk about everything, since he just told them about Teresa and knew they were so overwhelmed.

They finally came out of their room, went downstairs and hugged their dad. Crying, he said, "I am sorry for not telling you all about me and your mom. We can get through this together. Let's pray." "I believe that no weapon that is formed against me or my family shall prosper…Lord I humbly submit to you father for I know I cannot protect my family adequately…but you can protect us O Lord in Jesus name defend us O Lord in Jesus name Shield us O Lord in Jesus name." The twins said together, "Tell mom we miss her and love her. Amen." He told the twins, "Always be truthful and love the person you are with when you get older, because that is what I didn't do. I love your mom, but I wasn't truthful with her." The twins looked at their dad and agreed with tears coming down their faces. Richard continued to hug them, and they went into the living room to watch TV. Richard's phone went off, but he didn't answer. He saw who it was and pushed decline. Richard continued to spend time with the twins watching TV, playing board games, and eating pizza.
Three hours later his phone rang again, but this time he answered. It was George. "Hey Richard, how are you doing?" Richard answered with an attitude, "Fine."

"Are you okay?"

"Yes."

"Well, I was calling you to tell you I'm sorry for what I said about Teresa. I shouldn't have bought it up, but I just wanted to let you know what I heard. When that happened, I was getting ready to go out of town, and I didn't know all that had occurred. I am so sorry. Richard responded, "No problem, man. I just didn't know how you knew so much. Seems like all that wasn't in the newspaper are on the news." "Well, you know how people talk. I work around a lot of different people, so that is how I know about everything." Richard said, "No problem." He thought to himself, "Something about him I don't care for. Hmm." "Well brother, I also wanted to ask you…"

"What now?" George said, "You sound like I am getting on your nerves."

"I'm okay."

"Who was that man that was walking up and down in front of the church street quoting bible verses?"

"That is the ex-pastor, Vincent." George asked, "What happened to him?"

"Well, he had a big megachurch around the corner, and he led the people the wrong way."

"Do you mean he was living a lie and wasn't truthful with his members?" Richard responded, "Yes, so now he just wears his church robe with the Bible in his hand. He's been doing that for years. The bishop has been trying to get him to come in, but he will not. His whole family goes there now, even his members that used to belong to his church."

"Man, that is sad."

"But when he gets ready, the church doors are always open. Only you know when you get sick and tired of being sick and tired. Everybody's salvation is their own, even you, George." Laughing, George said, "Well I'm not ready to let go and let God."

"Okay, you have a blessed night. I have to go to work tomorrow."

"I understand, Richard. Well, if you need anything, I'm just a phone call away."

"I know. Have a blessed night. Bye, George." George hung up the phone and started to laugh out loud.

At the prison, 1 week later....

Sister was giving the word while Big Lee sat back and listened. When it was over, all the inmates were shouting, "Hallelujah. Thank you, God, for saving me, Amen." Big Lee walked up and said, "Praise the Lord, Sister. Praise the Lord," while clapping his hands. Sister thanked Big Lee and he said, "You're welcome." Sister asked, "How are you today?"

"I am blessed after that sermon you just gave."

"Thanks, Big Lee."

"I have something for you in your cell."

"Oh no, you don't have to do that."

"You have been a blessing to everyone in here, so it is time for you to receive." Big Lee smiled at her.

"Why me?"

"Why not you, sister?"

"Thanks."

"No problem. Trust me, no problem." He walked away and continued to do his job. Sister said to herself, "God, thank you for this man. He has been truly nice to me, but I don't understand why. Why isn't he doing the same thing for the other women?" She was puzzled.

Some months later, George called Richard. "Hey Richard, just checking back with you to see if you have any work. I am trying to buy this building to start my own company. I have been saving up so I can purchase the building." Richard asked, "What kind of business?"

"A cleaning business."

"Are you still at your night job?"

"Yes. I am still there."

"Okay, but I don't have any work for you. I have a full staff. I told you I would let you know when I have something."

"Okay, Richard."

"By the way George, we are having a revival all this month for healing and deliverance. I would like for you to come."

"Thanks, but no thanks and anyway, your church can't even heal or deliver the ex-pastor that has been wearing a church robe for years. What is up with that Richard?"

"The doors are always open for anyone to come through it."

"Well, I don't think I have enough money for the church." He started to laugh. "It's not about that George. The bishop and the members have helped my family through so much and are still helping us. "Well, I am one of them that will not be coming through those doors again."

"That is your choice. You have a blessed day, George."

"Have a nice day."

Richard hung up the phone. He prayed, "God, is there something going on with this man? I don't know, but I am getting bad vibes from him. Am I wrong God? If I am God, I am truly sorry." He just shook his head.

8

It was the first day of the Revival. The twins were getting ready for a day of praise and worship when they approached their dad and said, "Dad, we have been praying to God and we forgive you for what you did to our mom. We love you."

Richard started crying and hugging them, while he shouted, "Thank you, God! Thank you, God!" He told them, "I love you so much and whenever you need me, let me know. If I make a mistake and say something that hurts your feelings, please let dad know. If someone else says something or tries to do something to you, let daddy know. I am here to protect you at all times." The twins looked at their dad. Crying, they gave him a big hug saying, "We know dad. We love you so much!" Richard smiled and with tears coming down his face said, "I love you too! Now, let's get ready for church!"

In the car, Justin said, "Praise the Lord!" Justice said, "Amen." Richard laughed, "Amen! Amen, kids!" When they got to church, they saw Vincent walking up and down the street. Justice said, "Dad, why won't he come on in?" Richard answered, "We asked him, but he just keep walking up and down the street."

"But God forgives us when we make mistakes, right?"

"Yes, He does forgive us, but Vincent has to forgive himself." When they entered the church, the members were shouting, "Hallelujah! Hallelujah! Praise God." People were getting healed and delivered. Bishop Mike II started preaching, "Yes,

God. Only you can fix the broken. We Know that God is the one and only perfect Father. We all fall short of His Glory. God is the only loving, caring, and forgiving God. God said knock and He will answer. Are we knocking?" A member of the church said, "Bishop, yes." "God doesn't ask for much. He just wants us to love and obey. We all go through storms, but the storms are not to weaken us. They are to build us up. Just like when we go to the gym. We are working out trying to get that high school weight back, right?" Everyone started laughing saying, "Amen, Bishop."

"I have been trying to get that figure back on a treadmill with a cupcake in my hand." Everyone laughed. "But church, what I am saying is when you go through a storm in your life, it is not to bring you down. It's to build you up. Occasionally we have storms that are longer than others. That is because God is preparing you for what God has for you. We go through storms sometimes just to help someone else from what they are dealing with." All you could hear was shouting, crying, and people speaking in tongues. Bishop continued, "Is there anyone that has not given their life to God?" Fifteen people got saved and this went on for weeks. Everyone was crying and praising God as they left the church. The bishop saw Richard and the twins, he asked. "How are you and the twins doing?" Richard responded, "Thanks to the Almighty, you, and the members, we are blessed." Smiling, he said, "We have our moments. Well, we had a lot of moments."

"Just keep reading your word and praying. God will heal you all, but it is going to take time. We just have to leave it all at His feet." Amen." Bishop noticed Vincent still walking up and down the street. He said, "Pastor, you are welcome to come in whenever you want to." Vincent just keeps walking up and down the street. His family approached the bishop and said, "We tried to get him to come in. It's just like he doesn't hear us." "God hasn't given up on him. He has given up on himself. God will heal him, but he has to forgive himself first."

"Amen, you are truly right, bishop." Now everyone has left the church but Vincent. It is Saturday, one more day of revival.

Last day for Revival, Sunday morning....

Richard and the twins got out of the car and saw Vincent. The twins said, "Dad, is Mr. Vincent ever going to come in the church?" "Everybody has been trying to get him to come in, but he just won't." Justin and Justice walked over to Vincent and both of them grabbed him by his hands and said, "God forgives you." Vincent just looked at them and started to cry. He clearly said Amen and walked in the church with the twins. Justin held one hand and Justice held the other. Vincent walked in saying, "Thank you, Lord." His clothes were torn and very filthy. Vincent had so much dirt on his face and body you could hardly recognize him.

The Bishop said, "Yes, Lord." He was preaching from Luke 15:11-32 about the prodigal son. "Yes, he asked his dad for all his inheritance, not a little of it, but all his inheritance. Can I get an Amen? Church, when we think about our Father, you can always come back. He doesn't care what you did. God loves us just for who we are. Amen, church?"

Everyone cried out in joy. Vincent knelt down in front of the pulpit while his family was kneeling and praying that God be with him. After Vincent and his family got up from kneeling down, he turned around to address the members of the church. He had something he wanted to tell them. Vincent said, "But God.

You may have heard my story, but you do not know my story." He told them that he used to be a pastor of a megachurch Vincent continued, "I talked the talk, but did not walk the walk. I was honestly living a lie and made so many mistakes in my life….wasn't truthful to my family members. Instead of me being in the world, I was of the world." Everyone cried and praised God. He told them that God had truly blessed him to be a pastor. "I thought it was just a title, but it was much more than that." "Took advantage of it until I couldn't manipulate it anymore, hurt a lot of people, family, friends, and most of all my beautiful wife. I was smiling on the outside and crying on the inside. Didn't realize how much I was hurting until I saw it on the faces of the people that love me." Vincent continued, thought I was a locksmith, started opening doors that should've stayed closed. It would have been better, "just to wait on God to open them. I used to be gay, until God showed me that it wasn't who He wanted me to be. So, I had to realize that God had forgiven me a long time ago. I knew the bible from front to back, but I didn't know God in my heart, as tears rolled down his face. I didn't forgive myself until these two beautiful angels walked up to me and grabbed my hands and said, God forgives you. So, what I am saying to the church is, it does not matter what you have done. God will always be there. We all fall short from his Glory."

After that, so many people walked up to the pulpit to get saved. They have never seen this many people get saved at their church. People from all over the world came to this revival. Vincent and his family reunited and went home. He told his family how much he loved them, and appreciated them for never giving up on him.

9

Vincent became a man of God again and started going to Bishop Mike II's church. He went to every bible study and even joined the choir, where he met a beautiful woman named Elizabeth. They became good friends, and she went to every doctor's appointment with him. They even started riding to church together. She also decided to take Vincent shopping for some new clothes and shoes. They started developing feelings for each other and Vincent wanted to marry her but….he had to talk to Lisa first about signing the divorce papers.

Vincent visited Lisa to tell her how sorry he was for ruining her life and asked her to forgive him for all he had done. Lisa said, "I forgave you a long time ago because that is what God did for me." They both cried, hugged each other, and said I love you.

"I met a lady at the church," Vincent finally said.

"I already know about her because God put it in my spirit. You have my blessing. I signed the divorce papers a long time ago, so you can go on and marry her." She then told him, "Have a blessed life and I will see you again in heaven."

George called Richard. Richard looked at his phone and said, "I don't have time for George's negativity." He then decided to answer. "Hello, George."

"Hello, brother. How are you doing?"

"Blessed."

"I just wanted to tell you my good news." Richard responded, "What? You got saved?"

"Yeah, right. No, I bought that building I was telling you about. The one I was saving up for my cleaning business."

"That's good. Well, George, you caught me at a bad time. I'm doing something right now."

"Well, I'm getting ready to go out of town so I can sign the paperwork."

"Okay, good luck with your business," and then Richard hung the phone up without saying goodbye. George looked at the phone smiling and said, "He could at least tell a brother bye."

At the Prison....

After the women finished eating their meal, they went to the recreation room to watch TV. Some of the ladies chose to play games. Sister was reading her bible when Big Lee walked over to her to say hi. Sister said to him, "Thanks for the lip gloss. I needed it. I was using butter from the kitchen."

He told her, "I know. That is why I bought you some." She smiled at him. He then told her, "I got you. Whatever you need and I also left you something in your cell again." She smiled and said to him, "You are truly a blessing. No one has ever given me this much attention, even. "My ex-spouse never did this. It's the little things that matter." She started blushing as he smiled at her. It was time for the women to get back to their cells. She looked under the mattress and there were chocolate bars. Her cellmate Brenda said, "Sister, I think he really likes you. Every time he comes to work, he has something for you." Sister smiled at Brenda. "Since he's the Big Baller shot caller, maybe he can get a cell phone up in this joker and a TV." They both started laughing. Sister said, "That would be nice."

"Sister, I told you, you still got it." Sister started laughing out loud. The other C.O. told them to shut up and go to bed. Sister and Brenda started saying their prayers before they went to bed when Big Lee heard the other C.O. yell at them. He told him he needed to calm down and "The one in that cell is all mine." The other C.O. told Big Lee, "Man, I am sorry about that."

"Be careful." "Man, she is an inmate. She isn't going anywhere. She is here for a while." Big Lee told him, "I do not care. Like I said, leave that one alone." The C.O. kept apologizing to him as he turned around to walk away from Big Lee. So then he went back to Sister cell to make sure she was okay before his shift had ended to tell her bye and that he was going to clock out and will talk to her tomorrow. After he left

Brenda said girl I don't know what you did to this man but he is all over you like white on rice. They both start laughing, then she said to Sister maybe. I need to put more butter on my lips like you do laughing out loud. Sister told her it's not the butter that got his attention, it's the beauty. Brenda then said well maybe if I had got plastic surgery like you did. He would be checking me out to smiling, but I was already gorgeous before the plastic surgery. Now what do you have to say Miss. Brenda?

They laughed so hard at each other until tears just started to roll down their faces. Sister told her I'm not going to be up all night with your foolishness. Then they hugged each other, smiled, said their prayers and went to sleep.

10

Weeks and months passed by and Big Lee was still making sure Sister was okay. They began to get closer. He started sitting in on every Bible study she had with the inmates. Every time they had church, Big Lee was there. He did not care what the other C.O.s said. He still did what he wanted to do, just like he told her. He was running the prison, and everybody was scared of him. He was 6 feet 9 inches tall looking like a bodybuilder, with a beard and medium-length hair. He was a very attractive man. All the inmates liked him, but he had his eyes on one woman…. Sister. This went on for a long time until she started having feelings for him.

Brenda told Sister, "I see you, Sister. Next thing you know, he will be asking you to marry him and have his kids." The two women started laughing. Brenda told her again to ask Big Lee if he could get a phone. Sister said, "I am not going to ask him that." "Why not? He is doing everything else. You might as well use it before you lose it."

"Girl, you are crazy." Brenda said, "I am not that crazy. I'm trying to get a phone up in here."

"I don't know about that."

"I can call my family and you can too."

"I don't think my family would want to hear from me."

"I don't know why not. You have changed your life and ours too. Before you came, I was getting into fights all the time with the inmates. I was the top dog here. Now, I just want to learn more about God. I always stayed in the hole. Now, I am working in the kitchen and so are the other women." Sister said, "All the glory goes to God."

"Well, if you didn't teach us about the Glory, we probably would be killing each other. You need to take the credit for that." "I can't take credit for what God has done in your lives." They heard footsteps and hurried to lay down like they were asleep. It was Big Lee. He said, "Oh, now you all are going to act like you are asleep." They looked up and saw who it was. He said, "It's okay." They all started laughing. He said, "Sister, here is something for you." He gave her some apples and oranges and then told her he was going to clock out and go home. "I've been thinking about you a lot." She smiled at him and said, "Thanks."

Brenda waited until he left and said to Sister, "Girl, I told you we can get a phone out of that joker."

"Don't call him that. He's a good man."

"I am just saying, Sister. You must have forgotten about the game." "No, I didn't forget. I just don't play the games anymore. That is what got me in here."

"He could get it for me and a flat screen TV." Sister started laughing, "Brenda girl, you are so silly, that is why I love you so much."

"Do you love me enough to get me a cell phone and a flat screen TV?" Sister laughed and told Brenda, "I'm going to sleep." "While you're sleeping, think about it."

The next day they did the same routine. Sister looked around for Big Lee but didn't realize he was off duty. Brenda whispered in her ear, "You looking for your prison husband?" Sister started laughing and said, "Girl, you are so silly."

"I'm not lying."

"No, you're not. I guess he didn't have to work today."

After they ate breakfast, one of the C.O.s gave her a note from Big Lee. It said that he took a couple of days off to take care of something that he was doing for her. Sister showed Brenda the note and Brenda said, "I told you he was your prison husband."

"No, he's not." Brenda asked, "What could he possibly be doing for you? Doesn't he know this is your home now?" Sister laughed and said, "I'm sure he does. He should know. He works here." They both started laughing. "Girl, I don't know about this one. He looks so good. He should be able to get any woman he wants. Maybe you are the one for him."

"Me and him can't have a future with each other."

"I don't know, Sister. Maybe he sees something we don't."

"Maybe."

They started walking to their cell when Brenda said, "He can have me anyway he wants to. It's been a long time since I had my oil changed. Hasn't it been a long time since you had one too?" Brenda started laughing.

"God is my man."

"He is mine too, but there's nothing wrong with a little dessert."

"Girl, you're so crazy. I love you because you keep it real."

"That's the only way I know." They both smiled.

11

Big Lee returned to work and saw Sister and Brenda going outside with the other women. Brenda joked with Sister, "There goes your release."

"What are you talking about now?" Release you from all that is built up inside of you," and they both started laughing. Big Lee asked, "How are you all doing?" They both said, "Fine." Then Brenda said, "Fine, just like you look Big Lee." She threw back her hair and smiled at him. Big Lee said, "You know I only have eyes for Sister, but she doesn't like me like that." Sister smiled. "I have something for you."

"I told you. You don't have to do this."

"I told you that you deserve everything I give you and more." Sister smiled and said, "Okay, thanks again for doing these things for me but the other ladies are getting jealous."

"So, they will be okay."

Later that day, he gave sister some oranges and chocolate. When she was in her cell, Brenda told her, "See what I told you? You might as well get the cell phone and flat screen TV."

"Now you know they are not going to let that happen."

"Well, he is doing everything else. I'm just making sure you dot all your I's and cross your T's."

"Brenda, I don't know what I'm going to do with you." Sister grabbed one of the oranges and asked Brenda if she wanted one. Brenda declined, "I'm still trying to digest that lumpy oatmeal from this morning."

"Yeah, that was some pretty bad oatmeal." Sister thought about it, "Brenda, didn't you cook that oatmeal?" Brenda busted up laughing.

Later that night, Sister complained about having stomach pains. Brenda told the C.O. and he told her to go back to bed, "Sister will be alright." Suddenly, they heard someone else. It was Big Lee. By this time Sister was bent over holding her stomach. He asked Brenda, "What's wrong?" She said, "All of a sudden, Sister started complaining that her stomach was hurting. I thought it was gas from my oatmeal earlier." Big Lee started laughing. Sister told him, "Stop laughing, nothing is funny."

"Let me take you to the nurse's station." By this time, Sister could barely walk. Brenda said, "Sister, I will pray that you will be okay. After she ate that orange you gave her, a few hours later, she was complaining."

Big Lee said, "I got her."

"I am glad I didn't eat one."

Big Lee passed the nurse's station, when Sister said, "Where are you going?" He said, "She looks like she needs to go to the hospital."

"You are going to get into trouble." Big Lee told her, "Anything for you, Sister." By this time, they had made it to his truck and Sister was passed out. He put her in the back seat so no one would see her. When he got to the gate, the officer asked, "Why are you leaving early?"

"The alarm went off at my house. I will be right back," Big Lee said coolly. "I'll see you when you get back and have the other officer on duty to cover for you."

The next morning at the prison they were making their rounds to check on the inmate, they noticed that Sister was not in her cell. They asked Brenda where Sister was. She said that Sister was sick last night and Big Lee told her he was going to take her to the nurse, but she never came back. I asked the other C.O where was Sister? When I woke up in the middle of the night because I was worried about her, he told me to go back to bed."

After they found out that Sister was missing, the C.O closed all the cell doors and sounded the alarm. They looked everywhere, but couldn't find them.

The warden told one of the C.O.s to bring Brenda to his office so he could talk to her about what happened. She told the warden that Big Lee was supposed to be taking Sister to see the nurse last night after she got sick. It was hours later after eating an orange that he had given to Sister. The C.O. took Brenda back to her cell, and put a manhunt out on them.

It was on the news and in the newspaper. The policemen went to Big Lee's house and surrounded it. They told them to come out. There was no response. They kicked the front and back doors in. There was no Big Lee or Lisa. They told the public if they see them, they should call the police immediately because they're both dangerous.

12

When Lisa finally woke up, Big Lee was punching her in the face and had burnt her with cigars. She began crying and screaming for Big Lee to stop when she noticed that she was tied to a beam. She did not know where she was. But, she did see the windows painted black and heard water dripping. Also, she saw big rats running around. All the while, Big Lee stood there smiling. Lisa kept begging and pleading for him to stop, but Big Lee had so much anger in him. She did not understand why he was doing this. She cried and screamed because of the unbearable pain. Blood dripped down her face. No one heard her because the only thing around was railroad tracks. Lisa kept praying to God for Big Lee to stop, but he didn't.

Lisa asked, "Why? What have I done to deserve this?" Tears were running down her face. He continued punching her. All of a sudden, he stopped and sat in a chair directly in front of her. He told Lisa that he needed a lunch break. "Why are you doing this to me? I thought you were taking me to the hospital," said Lisa. Big Lee laughed, "Yeah right, more like to the morgue. This is the only place I was taking you."

Lisa kept crying and pleading over and over again, "Why are you doing this to me? I never did anything to you. Please let me go, please." At this point, Lisa had blood all over her face and burn marks all over her body. Lisa eventually started praying to God that Big Lee would let her go again. Lisa didn't understand why Big Lee would hurt her. This continued for days. He refused to let her use the restroom and didn't give her anything to eat, all the while he sat there eating in her face. Finally, she asked him for some water and food. Big Lee responded, "You don't deserve anything."

"What did I do to you? I thought you liked me."

"Yes, until I got you out of prison." Lisa still prayed to God for him to let her go.

He told her, "God isn't going to save you now. God may have healed you from AIDS, but he can't heal you from this bullet that has your name on it."

Lisa asked him again and again, "Why Big Lee?" Big Lee said, "Do you really want to know why I am doing this to you?" Crying, she said, "Please." Big Lee went to the restroom. When he returned, Lisa saw that he had shaved off his hair and bread. He looked at her with so much hatred in his eyes. He said, "Just call me Revenge. Do you remember now, Ivy?"

Lisa said, "Oh my God, George. I am so sorry for what I did to you." "It is too late now, Ivy. I lost everything. My wife, my kids, and my soul left when my family left. I went back to school just to get revenge on you. I knew that was the only way I could get close to you, and I also know the warden. I was fortunate that they needed C.O.s badly at the prison because most of them were fired because of the way they treated the inmates. They did not even do a background check on me. So, lucky me. Now it is your turn to die like your friend, Envy." Lisa kept begging for him to not kill her.

He said, "Not now. I am enjoying what I'm doing right now, maybe later. You are going to feel my pain after all these years." After some time had passed, he decided to let her go to the restroom. He said, "You are smelling up my building."

When he untied her from the beam, she noticed a light coming from a crack below the door. She decided to run. He saw her. "If you take one more step, I will shoot you."

She stopped dead in her tracks and turned around to look at him. Then he said, "You know what? I am going to shoot you anyway." George pulled the trigger, and nothing happened. The gun jammed. He looked over her head and saw a big bright light that looked like an angel.

While George was distracted, Lisa turned back around and started running again. He ran behind her, but he tripped and fell. He couldn't catch her. Lisa ran until she came across a policeman. She told him everything that happened and where George was located. He called for backup and the police surrounded the building. While they searched the building, a helicopter was surveilling from above. There was no George to be found. Then the police went to his house again. They yelled for him to come out, but no response. Than broke the door down and searched his house. The police did not find any traces of George. Reporters began camping out in front of

George's house. He was on every news channel and newspaper all over the world. They had an all points bulletin out on him deemed armed and dangerous, urging the public to report any sightings immediately." and still no George.

They went to every employer that was on record. Then they finally went to Richard's office to let him know who George truly was. The officer said, "George was the one that killed your wife." Richard became angry, "George worked for me but I didn't know he was the killer. I was wondering why he knew so much about her death. Now I know." Richard not only felt angry, but he also felt foolish and betrayed all over again.

The officer said, "We are doing everything in our power to find him." Richard said, "I am too." He grabbed his gun and began to leave. The officer stopped him and said, "Let us handle it. We will find him, Richard." Richard replied, "Not if I find him first."

The officer reminded him, "You have to be here for the twins." Richard broke down to his knees and started crying. One of the officers knelt and put his arms around him and said, "We are going to catch him. I promise you that." After the officers had left he got up and sat at his desk with the gun saying how he was going to find George himself, and told his secretary he was leaving for the rest of the day. He drove around the city to see if he could find him. For hours with his gun on the set crying and shaking his head saying over and over again how it was. George fought that his wife is dead, and what he was going to do when he found him. George was nowhere to be found so Richard decided to just go home. Tried to call him, but went straight to voicemail, shaking his head as tears rolled down Richard's face. He stayed up all night watching their wedding video and looking at pictures, crying and talking to himself, about how he did not protect his wife like a real husband was supposed to.

13

Months passed and no George. Richard sat in front of George's house for a month straight. He didn't go to work and had one of his employees take care of his daily duties. The twins had no idea what was going on. Richard just told them he was working late. He even kicked George's backdoor in at one point and still no George.

One day, new neighbors with kids moved in next to George. The kids were outside playing ball and it accidentally went into George's yard. One of the kids went into the yard to retrieve the ball. When the child looked up, he saw a man looking out the window. The man closed the curtain quickly. This scared the children, and they ran home. The child told his parents because they were told no one lived there. The parents called the police who had a suspicion it was George.

They surrounded the house and asked him to come out. No response. They broke the door down and noticed someone was living in the house. They searched the house from top to bottom. Then an officer noticed that a rug was folded over on the floor. He moved the rug and discovered a door to a hidden room under the house. They opened the door and yelled for George to come out or they were coming down shooting. George finally came out with his hands up, smiling at them, and they threw him to the floor.

Laughing, George said, "It is about time you all did something right I had to do your job." They cuffed him and read him his miranda rights, and took him to jail.

14

Two months later George had a court date, and the Judge heard all the witness statements and asked the lawyer how he pleads. He said, "Guilty."

The Judge sentenced him to death by injection. The judge asked George, "Is there anything you would like to say to the families?"

"No," smiling. He then laughed as he said, "I died a long time ago." All over, people were crying, even the reporters. Once George was transferred to the prison, they took him to his cell. George started talking to his cellmate. The cellmate asked, "What happened in court?"

"I was sentenced to lethal injection. I told them I died a long time ago when that happened to me. What did they expect a brother to do, just let it go? Are they out of their mind? Those things were out there trying to infect everyone. If I did not work with Teresa's husband, I would have never known who they were. They should have just dealt with their husbands. I did not do this to them. So what, I like to go out and cheat every now and then. Does that mean I have to die from it?"

George looked at his cellmate and wondered why he was laughing and why the C.O.s was still standing there laughing too. He asked, "What's so funny?" They all looked at his bed and there were oranges and apples on it.

"Who did this?" No one answered. George asked again with rage in his eyes and in his voice, "WHO DID THIS?" They started laughing even louder. George looked over at his cellmate and the other C.O.s. He proceeded to punch his cellmate in the face and knocked him completely out.

"Now that is funny!" George said. The C.O.s begin to grab George and throw him on the floor. They handcuffed him and as they took him away to the hole, George was still laughing. The C.O. told him that he better hope his cellmate doesn't die. George said "What are they going to do to me? I'm already dead!" As he smiled and said, "send him a fruit basket and tell him it's from me." Then he started to laugh as the C.O.s proceeded to throw him in the hole. George shook his head.

Two weeks later one of the C.O.s went to George's cell to tell him his cellmate died. He laughed and said well it looks like I'll be seeing him again. We are going to be hell mates. The C.O. looked at George, and said " you are crazy for real man." Then he hurried up to close the cell door.

After Lisa got out of the hospital. The C.O took her back to prison, and she started to tell the ladies what happened to her. The inmates said they wondered why he took to her like he did, knowing the reasons why she was in prison. Brenda said, "I am glad he did not try to clean my pipes." Then the other inmates started to laugh at her. Lisa told Brenda, "It's not funny."

"I am sorry, Sister. I was just saying. You know I was trying hard to get with him too." Then Lisa started laughing, and gave her a hug. Lisa continued to talk to them until they told her that her lawyer was waiting to see her. When she got to the room, he told her, "George was sentenced to death. The judge pushed your date back some because of what George did to you, but you are still on Death Row."

"I understand. It is my fault that George did what he did. So, whatever comes to me, I am okay. I am at peace with it." She left the room and started crying. "God, I knew this day was coming. I am ready. Thanks for healing and covering me still after all the harm I caused." The C.O. took Lisa back to her cell where she stayed for the rest of the day and prayed.

15

Five Months Later....

Richard went to the prison to see George and asked, "Man, what is wrong with you? Why did you kill my wife? If I was anything like I used to be in the past before. I got delivered, your ass would've been tied to a cement block in the ocean getting eaten by piranha. You were wrong for what you did George! You better be glad they caught you before I did. No wonder you knew so much about my wife's death."

George started, laughing in Richard's face, said, "Man, you are crazy." Richard was so mad he tried to break the glass window with the phone. George continued to laugh at Richard, "Are you finished?"

"No! Why would you even come back to work for me man?"

"Now it is my turn. I want to see you suffer. I just want to look in your eyes and see your pain. Your dead ex-baby's momma was out there giving anybody and everybody that deadly disease. Did you think she was going to keep getting away with it, brother? Are you crazy? I lost everything because of them and now it was their time. I didn't care what price it cost. Now I am done. You have a blessed day."

Richard had so much fire in his eyes. George smiled and hung up the phone and walked away. Richard sat there for a minute talking to God. "I made this big mess. My wife would still be here if I wasn't thinking with my other head. I am sorry again, God." Richard finally got up with tears rolling down his face shaking his head.

Later that week, it was time for George's sentencing. They gave him his last meal. Once he was finished, the officer on duty came and got him. He walked George down the long hallway and into the execution chamber without saying a word. The officer told him to lay down on the bed and asked him if he had any last words. George said, "I would not have done anything different," and smiled.

They administered the lethal injection, only he didn't die, George looked at them out of breath and said is that all you got smiling. They had to do it again.

16

Four Years Later....

It was Lisa's turn to walk down the long hallway to the execution chamber, but before they took her, all the inmates hugged her and told her how much they loved her. She said to them, "Once you get out, please do not come back. Don't take things into your own hands. Let God fight your battles and stay in the word. Don't stop praying."

Then they took her away. They asked Lisa what she wanted for her last meal. She smiled a little bit and said, "I know one thing. I don't want any oranges."

She ate her last meal, and the officer came and got her. Once in the execution chamber, she lay down and they asked her for her last words. Crying, she said, "Please tell the families that I am so sorry for what I did."

They gave her the injection. She died minutes after, not like George. They had to up his dosage.

As for the rest of the men they had infected. They didn't know who they were at the time. The only reason George knew was because he worked with Teresa's husband, Richard.

The other men didn't know until it was on the news, and in the newspapers. There were so many people that got hurt by what Lisa and Teresa did. You really never know a person just by looking at their outside appearance. They were so pulchritude and took advantage of it. "Every man that saw Lisa and Teresa really lusted after them."

Romans 12:19-21 (KJV) Dearly beloved, avenge not yourselves, but rather give place unto wrath: for it is written, Vengeance is mine; I will repay, saith the Lord. Therefore if thine enemy hunger, feed him; if he thirst, give him drink: for in so doing thou shalt heap coals of fire on his head.

Ephesians 6:12
For our fight is not
against flesh and blood,
but against principalities,
against powers, against the
rulers of the darkness of
this world, and against
spiritual forces of evil in
the heavenly places.

Note from the Author

I hope that everyone who reads these two fiction books know that God is truly real. God just wants us to love Him and obey Him. God will never force anything on you, but God will never leave you nor forsake you.

Thanks for the support of everyone who purchases my books. To my sons Michael Jr. and Shayeen Edwards for helping me with the book cover and title. Michelle Kristin for editing. I would also like to thank Nace V. Sayles, the artist that drew the portrait on the book cover of my vision for Retaliation II. Again, thank you Michael Jr. for doing the background of the book covers.

Retaliation

II

www.ingramcontent.com/pod-product-compliance
Lightning Source LLC
Chambersburg PA
CBHW070655010826
48975CB00013B/1305